The Football Boy Wonder

Martin Smith

For Natalie and Emily.

CONTENTS

ACKNOWLEDGMENTS

Charlie Fry and his footballing adventure is a story that I've pondered for a long time.

It's taken years to find the right words to bring Charlie's story to life. I hope you enjoy reading it as much as I have writing it.

Naturally, I could not have written this book without the help of numerous people.

In no particular order, I would like to thank:

My wife Natalie for her kindness, patience and determination. She is, as always, my rock.

Sam Boniface for volunteering to proofread The Football Boy Wonder, kindly giving up her weekends to ensure my love of commas did not ruin the book.

My nephew Tom Smith for providing valuable feedback that helped to structure the book's crucial middle section.

Mark Newnham for creating a brilliant cover – and then steadfastly refusing to take any credit. He'll hate this mention but life is tough.

And finally, those people who made Hall Park such an undiscovered football mecca in the 1990s. If you've ever mentioned the immortal phrase "Tree Factor!" then you are, and always will be, one of us.

1. THE MISKICK

The ball flew high into the air, swirling in the blustery wind. The crowd and players all raised their heads to follow its direction.

Everyone except for one person.

Charlie Fry jumped up and down on the spot standing on the sidelines trying to keep calm as he waited to come on as a substitute.

He was nervous enough to be sick, but he hoped that no-one else would realise how scared he was.

He had been thinking about this moment for two weeks – his school's long-awaited home match against their title rivals North Street.

Wearing the school's all-white kit, Charlie looked around as his teacher Mr Dickens signalled to the referee that Blackfriars wanted to make a change.

Ignoring his shaking hands and hiding them deep inside his long shirt sleeves, Charlie gulped in air as he felt the first drops of rain begin to fall.

It looked as if the whole school had turned out to watch on the playing field. Charlie knew his mum and dad were out there somewhere too watching his big moment.

When he was sitting on the substitutes' bench during the first half, the crowd didn't look so big.

Now standing on the touchline alongside Mr Dickens waiting to go onto the pitch, it looked massive.

Charlie took a final puff on his trusty blue inhaler and threw it on the ground, seeing it land near the rest of his kit.

Making a final check to ensure his shin pads were safely secured inside his socks, he was ready.

The score was 1-1 and there was still ten minutes to go.

The winner of the game would be crowned league champions.

Blackfriars only needed a point to win the league so the pressure was now all on the visitors – the team who had won the league for the past three years.

For Charlie and the rest of his school year, this was their final chance to win the league before they went to secondary school.

Seamus Houseman was the player being replaced, a bulky ginger boy who was destined to play in the top flight in football – if you listened to him, of course.

Charlie held out his hand as a muddy Seamus trudged off towards the bench, annoyed he had been chosen to be subbed.

Seamus ignored the offer of a handshake, scowled and whispered in Charlie's ear: "Don't mess this up, Fry."

Charlie's eyes widened but he said nothing. He was sure he could hear his stomach growling with nerves as he ran onto the pitch.

Mr Dickens had told him to play left back, one of the positions that meant Charlie would not have to run too far.

Charlie ran onto the pitch, giving an awkward smile to goalkeeper Joe Foster who gave him a big thumbs-up as encouragement.

Joe had been Charlie's best friend since preschool.

They did absolutely everything together. Joe had always played as a keeper and everyone knew he was really good too.

Charlie stood next to the young lad in the red strip that Seamus had been marking until this point.

Thankfully, he was only a centimetre or two taller than Charlie and was just as skinny.

They were easily the two smallest players on the pitch – so at least Charlie would have a chance against him.

North Street had a goal kick.

The ball was immediately floated in Charlie's direction. It went high into the air and both boys jumped for the header.

They missed it before turning and scampering after the ball, which trickled harmlessly out of play for a throw-in.

Already gasping for breath, Charlie looked around to mark the small winger again but he was nowhere to be seen.

North Street had changed their line-up: the small lad had now been moved into the centre-forward position.

It meant North Street's star striker Brian Bishop was playing on the right wing – and Charlie had to try and stop him.

Bishop was the same age as Charlie but was head

and shoulders above him in height and weighed a lot more too.

He was built like a tank.

For years, Bishop had given Blackfriars' defenders nightmares and now Charlie – with the butterflies increasing by the second – had to mark him.

The throw-in was cleared and the ball went up the pitch towards North Street's goal.

Charlie jogged alongside Bishop, keeping close enough to mark the striker but trying not to move too far up the pitch so he wouldn't have to run back a huge distance.

Then the inevitable happened.

The North Street goalkeeper, a big lad nicknamed Peppermint, snatched the ball from the air and immediately kicked it in Bishop's – and Charlie's – direction.

Watching the flight of the ball, Charlie moved positively to head it away.

He watched the ball in the air, jumped and … fell face first into the wet grass.

A strong but subtle elbow into his back from Bishop was enough to send Charlie sprawling.

He looked at the ref, who waved play on – assuming Charlie had simply fallen over rather than been fouled.

Completely unmarked, the striker raced onto the loose ball as Blackfriars' remaining defenders desperately tried to catch him.

Bishop was too quick though.

He strode into the penalty area, waited for Joe to come towards him before coolly slotting the ball to the keeper's right and into the empty net.

North Street was now winning 2-1 with only

minutes to go.

As Bishop wheeled away in celebration, Charlie arrived back at the edge of the penalty area panting for breath.

His white kit was dishevelled after Bishop had thrown him into the mud.

Joe fished the ball out of the net as North Street's entire team celebrated in the corner, a pile of red-shirted bodies with Bishop at the bottom.

No-one said a word to Charlie as he resumed his position.

None of the team even looked in his direction. He knew they were blaming him, unable to see Bishop's sneaky foul.

North Street's celebrations finally ended after several minutes with a bedraggled but jubilant Bishop finally coming up for air.

As he jogged past Charlie, he whispered with a little smile: "Unlucky, Titch."

Charlie's cheeks went red as he watched Bishop run towards his own half for the kick-off.

The elbow had been unseen by almost everybody, he had been sure that he was going to head that ball away until Bishop had cheated.

"Chin up Charlie," Joe shouted from behind him.

There were four minutes left and Blackfriars wouldn't let the league go without a fight.

North Street had dropped deeper and deeper, defending their lead with every one of their players staying in their own half.

That suited Charlie.

Bishop was now too busy worrying about defending rather than attacking.

It gave Charlie time and space.

He touched the ball a couple of times, passing to his teammates cleanly and without fuss.

Mr Dickens was enthusiastically encouraging his players from the sideline, urging the entire team to push forward and grab the goal that would secure them league title.

Charlie found himself spending almost his whole time in the opposition half as North Street tried to protect their valuable lead.

The rain was getting heavier, making the pitch slippery and more difficult to play on.

Only two minutes were remaining on the referee's watch when the ball was pumped into the North Street box.

It pinged around the six-yard box before agonisingly trickling away for a Blackfriars corner.

A North Street defender headed the corner out of the penalty area, straight to where Charlie was waiting on the edge of the box.

He didn't hesitate, bringing the ball neatly under control and slipping it straight to Blackfriars' team captain Adam Knight.

Adam took the ball, slipped past Bishop's clumsy attempt at a block and calmly launched a right-foot thunderbolt.

The ball smashed against the bar with Peppermint rooted to the spot, flying up and behind for a goal kick.

Like the rest of his team and the majority of the crowd, Charlie had his hands on his head. It had been so close.

He jogged over to give Adam a friendly slap on the back.

"Unlucky, Ad. That was a great shot."

Adam shrugged off his hand and sneered: "That was a rubbish pass. Everyone knows I'm left footed and you passed it straight to my right.

"If we lose, Fry… this is your fault."

Charlie swallowed hard, fighting back tears. He knew as soon as Bishop had fouled him that he would be blamed for the result.

He jogged back to his position, refusing to even look at the rest of his teammates.

It was now deep into injury time with only seconds of the game remaining.

North Street's goal kick was over hit – going straight through to Joe, giving Blackfriars one final opportunity.

Joe's return kick was long, deep into the North Street half.

The ball was cleared partly but given only straight back to Blackfriars who were surging forward in numbers.

By now, every player – including Joe – was inside the North Street half.

Charlie was again hovering on the edge of the penalty area, the furthest player away from the action.

Then it happened.

Watching the ball on the far side of the pitch, Charlie began slowly moving towards the back post.

No one else was near him or paying him any attention. Everyone was concentrating on the ball.

As Charlie moved forward, the ball was crossed from the right wing, passing over the heads of everyone in the centre and sliding across the wet turf.

Charlie was unsure how he had got so deep inside the opposition's penalty area but there he was.

He was unmarked, running at top speed with the

ball zipping across the wet turf ahead of him – and coming in his direction.

It felt like everything was in slow motion. Suddenly the ball was in front of him.

Out of the corner of his eye, he could see Peppermint desperately scrambling across his goal to try and cover the danger.

But Charlie knew the keeper would not make it in time.

Charlie stuck out his right leg, sliding through the thick mud into the back of the net.

Lying tangled in the net, he waited for the eruption of cheers and his teammates to mob him in wild celebration.

The ref blew the final whistle and Charlie could hear the distant sound of people cheering nearby.

But something wasn't right.

He turned over and saw Adam, crouching down and staring at the ground crestfallen as jubilant North Street players celebrated around him.

Further back, Joe was squatting down in the centre circle unable to look up.

What had happened?

Charlie looked through the net and saw the muddy ball, innocently sitting the other side of the post. It hadn't gone in.

"Oh no," he groaned aloud.

Somehow he had missed.

Blackfriars had lost the league title by a single miskick.

☐

2. BLAMED

The Blackfriars football team were huddled in a circle listening to Mr Dickens' final team talk of the season.

His voice sounded like a frog, croaky after all the yelling during the match.

The teacher was trying to rally the team, who were taking the dramatic defeat badly.

He said: "This has been a great effort all season. You have done yourselves proud.

"Do not be too disappointed – you have been a great team and the school is honoured to be represented by such a bunch of talented footballers.

"We were unlucky today, that's all."

They had been true sportsmen – applauding the victorious North Street players, who were awarded the league trophy at the end of the game.

Bishop had held the trophy aloft, cheered loudly by his team and their parents.

The rest of the crowd clapped politely.

Covered from head to toe in mud, Charlie had shaken all of North Street's players' hands.

Many of the opposition had the kindness to mutter "unlucky" at his last minute effort.

Bishop had cuffed him round the head in a playful manner as they shook hands but said nothing more.

Their words meant nothing to Charlie, just like Mr Dickens' speech.

It was wasted on him.

Charlie felt hollow inside. Joe gave him a supportive clap on the shoulder as they walked towards the changing rooms.

"I was so close, Joe."

"I know. Next time, you'll definitely get there. When we go for Hall Park trials next month, you're going to have a blinder.

"I can feel it."

Charlie smiled weakly, knowing Joe was just trying to cheer him up.

He had almost no chance of being selected for Hall Park Rovers – their amateur local team – when the junior trials took place.

But he had to try.

The friends pushed open the door into the noisy home changing room.

But as soon as the door slammed closed, the room became deadly silent.

All that could be heard were the faint cheers coming from the celebrations in the away dressing room.

That made the situation even worse.

Adam, Seamus and another lad called Lee circled around Charlie, who had sat down on the bench to remove his filthy boots.

"Fry, you should have been playing netball with the rest of the girls today, not football," Adam taunted, causing the others to laugh.

Charlie blushed but kept silent.

"So how much did North Street pay you?

"Surely no-one can play that badly without doing it on purpose?"

Joe stepped in front of Adam.

The captain and the goalkeeper were nose-to-nose but there could be no mistake: Joe was easily the biggest person in the changing room.

"Shut up and back off.

"It wasn't his fault.

"Bishop pushed him before he scored.

"Everyone could see that.

"He nearly scored the equaliser and he set you up too!

"Shame you couldn't score when we needed you to."

Surprised by Joe's tone, Adam instinctively took a step back. Joe, by now, was red-faced with anger and he was wary of the burly goalkeeper.

Lee, a small lad with brown spiky hair and a missing front tooth, sneakily moved around Joe and began poking fun at Charlie's filthy strip.

"Ha. Old Charles has pooed his pants after missing that sitter!

"Look at the state of his kit!"

Several of the team sniggered at Lee's childish taunt. Charlie blushed at the pathetic insult but still remained silent.

He had spent years being taunted by Adam and the pack of schoolyard bullies.

He had always preferred to keep quiet rather than risk making them angry – and face further public humiliation.

He couldn't wait to start senior school in the autumn and get away from this bunch of idiots for good.

Joe, though, wouldn't let it drop.

He grabbed Lee's shirt and pushed him roughly away.

Shocked by the sudden movement, Lee squealed as he tumbled to the floor.

He bounced back up but stood behind Adam's shoulder, not wanting to have to confront Joe on his own.

Mr Dickens' arrival in the changing room ended the argument.

The others melted away, leaving Adam facing Joe and Charlie alone.

Keeping his voice low so the teacher could not hear him, he whispered: "We're not going to forget this, you little freak.

"You cost us the league title today, Titch.

"If I ever see you playing football again, I'll get you."

Looking Adam directly in the eye, Joe replied loudly so everyone could hear: "Say what you like. We don't care.

"Now… go away."

Adam moved back to the other side of the room as Mr Dickens heard Joe's loud words and moved closer to the small group, looking intently at Joe.

It was unusual for the goalkeeper to show such emotion.

Charlie took another puff on his inhaler, stored it in his backpack and nodded to his mate for his support.

He began hurriedly changing out of his strip,

hoping to get home as soon as possible so he could just be alone.

His hopes of winning the league – something that he had dreamt about for years – had turned into a complete nightmare.

3. LIGHTNING STRIKES

It was still raining when Charlie and Joe emerged from the changing rooms.

They had told their parents they would walk home together rather than get a lift and be forced to relive the agony of the game again.

The pair lived a street apart and had always been part of each other's families.

They walked in silence, mulling over the game and the argument with Adam and the team afterwards.

It was Joe who broke the silence.

"If this rain clears up, do you fancy a kick around later?

"I definitely need to practice catching crosses and one-on-ones – I still can't believe Bishop won that one."

He stopped himself, immediately aware that his words were only making Charlie's misery worse.

Charlie shook his head.

"No, I can't. I've got physio to do."

The reason Charlie struggled to run was because he had poorly lungs.

He had cystic fibrosis, which clogged up his lungs with a horrible sticky gunge.

It made it hard for him to breathe – and he was NEVER hungry.

He had to do physiotherapy each day and take a load of medicine too.

If he got too ill though, it almost always meant trouble. Even a simple cold usually meant a two-week stay in hospital.

Apart from the boring visits to hospital, Charlie didn't mind too much.

He had grown up with it and cystic fibrosis was simply part of his life.

It didn't stop him doing anything really but it did mean that he had to be a little bit more careful than most.

During his daily physio sessions, he always read football and adventure books on his tablet – the extra reading put him top of the class for English.

And he played video-games while doing his medicine morning and night, giving him plenty of practice to beat his friends.

More importantly, he could still play football, ride a bike or swim like the others.

He just needed to be careful about overdoing it.

Joe nodded, showing his understanding: "Oh yeah. What about tomorrow then?"

The following day was Saturday and the boys spent almost every weekend practising soccer skills at the Rec, the park that was two minutes from their house.

Sometimes they were joined by others but you could always rely on Joe, Charlie and their good friend Peter Bell to be kicking a ball around on the Rec.

"Sounds good," replied Charlie, wiping the rain out of his eyes.

The weather was getting worse – there was a thunderstorm coming.

He could feel his smartphone begin to buzz in his pocket.

They had reached the end of Joe's street, stopping on the corner as they finished their discussion.

"What shall we play?"

Joe grinned and rustled Charlie's short brown fuzzy hair.

"I reckon you probably need to practice headers and volleys."

Charlie punched his friend playfully on the arm but still managed a smile.

"Ha ha. That's not funny at all. I'll see you tomorrow."

They said goodbye with Joe sprinting the rest of the way to his driveway, scampering away to escape the bucketing rain.

He was inside within seconds.

Turning towards his own home, Charlie fished the ringing phone out of his coat pocket, answering a split second before it diverted to answerphone.

It was his mum panicking about Charlie being out in the bad weather.

He sighed.

"Yes, Mum. I'm fine, just at the end of Joe's street now.

"Okay, okay, Mum, I know I can't risk getting wet.

"Yes, I promise that I'm coming right now.

"I'll be home in two minutes – or maybe even less than that. Bye."

Charlie ended the call, shaking his head.

His mum worried way too much.

It was only a little bit of rain, after all.

A huge clap of thunder broke overhead.

It was followed immediately by a jagged bolt of lightning.

The storm was right overhead.

Perhaps his mum was right – it was worse than a few spots of rain.

The heavens opened. Charlie was getting soaked, his hair sticking flat to his head and the mud from the football pitch running into his eyes, making them sting.

He wiped his smartphone cover trying to keep it as dry as possible in the torrential rain.

The touchscreen mistook Charlie's intention – thinking he wanted to open an app instead.

The flick football app that he played every day popped up on the screen.

Charlie groaned and stopped walking.

All he wanted to do was to lock the phone, put it into his pocket away from the rain and get home, straight into a hot shower.

The app – one where you used your finger to direct a ball into the goal past various obstacles – was now in the process of opening.

Charlie moved the phone closer to his eyes, almost to the end of his nose, so he could see the screen clearly.

By now the rain had become so strong it was almost impossible to make out what was on the phone's screen.

Charlie flinched as an almighty thunderclap broke over his head.

Then his world went black.

4. HOSPITAL

Charlie looked at his mysterious surroundings.

He was in bed but it wasn't his bedroom.

He groaned silently.

He was in a hospital bed. But it was not his usual hospital though.

How on earth did he get here?

"Mum," he croaked, "where am I?"

His mum leaned forward, speaking quietly.

"Charlie? You're awake?"

"Oh, thank goodness for that. We have been so worried."

Her friendly face slowly came into focus. Her red eyes told him that she had been crying.

Charlie tried to sit up but his dad, sitting on the other side of the bed, put out a strong arm to keep his son lying down.

The door to the room opened and a middle-aged woman doctor marched in.

She seemed to be in a hurry, swiftly rummaging

through the file at the end of his bed and speaking quickly.

"How are you feeling, Charlie?"

Charlie screwed up his face. How did he feel? "I'm okay. Everything is a bit blurry though and my head really hurts."

The doctor replied: "Mr Fry, you're a very lucky boy. The lightning bolt must have struck within a few feet of you.

"Apart from a few nasty bumps and bruises, and that cut to your head, you seem fine.

"The double vision should ease over the next few days.

"We'll keep you in for observation overnight as a precaution but I fully expect you to be fine.

"Please take more care in thunderstorms in future."

She turned to Charlie's parents.

"If you have any further questions, please come and see me.

"I suggest you both return around tomorrow lunchtime.

"If there are no problems, he'll be fine to go home with you then."

The doctor reached the door, before turning and speaking to Charlie again.

"Oh, there's one more thing. You were very unlucky in the football game today.

"It was a great effort to try and reach that ball.

"If you show that type of determination in the future, you'll go a long way in life."

Charlie's dad answered for the family.

"You were at the game?"

She nodded, opening the door slightly.

"Yes, my son plays for North Street. He's the goalkeeper."

The doctor left the room, heading off to see the long list of patients on her evening round.

Charlie closed his eyes and flopped back onto his pillow.

The game had happened then – the league was still lost.

A small part inside of him had begun to hope that it had all been a dream.

Charlie opened his eyes again, confused.

"What happened to me, Dad?"

His father was a man of few words. Liam Fry was a builder, who loved football and horse-racing.

He was quiet but, when he spoke, his words were honest and accurate.

His dad paused briefly to find the right words and, when he spoke, his gentle voice was filled with concern.

"Son, it looks like you were hit by a lightning bolt. Obviously not a direct hit – thank God – but you were still close enough to absorb a lot of natural electricity.

"We think your phone took the brunt of it.

"We found burned out pieces of it scattered across the road.

"The doctor seems to think that the phone acted as some sort of conductor for the lightning – and pulled the electricity into you, sending you flying."

His dad stopped, finding the next words difficult to say.

"We heard the loud bang from our house.

"I ran out thinking there had been a car accident or something.

"That's when I saw you, just lying there in the garden of Mr and Mrs Espin.

"You were unconscious, I thought you were…."

His dad didn't finish the sentence.

He simply hugged his son, gripping him tightly to his wide chest.

His mum Molly did the same from the other side, until Charlie begged to be released before he was suffocated.

He felt exhausted again.

He had almost been hit by a bolt of lightning? How lucky had he been?

His vision was pretty bad.

He kept seeing strange floating shapes in front of his eyes.

It was not normal and it made him feel sick.

Charlie knew he needed some sleep. Everything would be fine in the morning.

With a bit of luck, he still might be able to meet Joe down the Rec for that kickabout.

"I'm tired, mum."

His mum smoothed his hair tenderly.

"I know, sweetheart. We'll go now and give you some rest.

"We'll be back first thing in the morning and get you home.

"We love you so much."

His mum turned and began to pick up their bags and coats, ready to leave.

Charlie's dad gave him a small squeeze on the shoulder and made his way to the door.

"Dad?"

His dad turned as he held open the door for Molly to leave first.

"Yes, Charlie?"

"Can I have a new phone please?"

His dad smiled and winked, following his wife out of the door and leaving Charlie alone in the dark.

5. STRANGE VISIONS

Charlie was allowed to leave hospital the next day but only after the woman doctor had given him and his parents some very strict instructions.

He had to rest for a week and was not allowed to play video games during that time.

Even worse, he couldn't play football, or any sport for that matter, for two weeks.

The Hall Park Rovers trials were due to take place in three weeks' time.

That gave him only seven days to get match fit and squeeze in some much-needed practice with Joe at the Rec.

It was going to be tight.

And he desperately needed to practice his heading and his shooting before the big day.

Charlie hadn't told anyone – not even Joe – but he was going to play as a striker at the trials.

He knew it was the most popular position in the team.

Everyone wanted to play up front and he didn't care about the intense competition.

This was his dream.

Charlie had always longed to be a centre-forward, banging in the goals and winning games for his team.

He had to try, at least.

And he wouldn't let some idiotic playground bullies, a crazy lightning bolt accident or a mystery floating shape in front of his eyes stop him from taking part in those trials.

At least he didn't have to go to school for a week under the doctor's orders.

It was the only bright spot in a rubbish week – it meant he wouldn't have to face Adam and the other goons for a while.

Perhaps they would forget about the game against North Street in that time although he knew he was being optimistic.

But his eyes were still struggling.

Thankfully, the double vision cleared up after his night in the hospital, when he kept dreaming about terrifying flashes of lightning.

But he kept seeing the same mystery object floating in front of his eyes whenever they were open.

It was bizarre – Charlie had never seen anything like it.

Whatever it was, the shape was definitely inside his head and not something anyone else could see, Charlie had decided.

He had made plenty of attempts to reach out and grab it but his fingers grasped thin air every time.

The object was a strange shape – a circle with a cross through the middle of it.

It was small and he could see through it without any difficulty but it still annoyed him.

What was it?

It disappeared whenever Charlie closed his eyes but, as soon as he opened them again, it was hovering somewhere in his vision.

Worried that the hospital staff would keep him in for further testing – or even worse think he was completely bonkers – Charlie didn't tell the doctors about the mystery object.

And he didn't dare to tell his parents either.

They were so happy to have him home he didn't have the heart to tell them that something was not quite right.

Even his little brother Harry was pleased to see him – stopping being his usual annoying self to give Charlie some peace and quiet.

Harry was space-obsessed as most six-year-olds are, so he would have probably blamed aliens if he had been told about the phantom shape.

But Charlie wouldn't be telling him about the shape either.

It wasn't only that though.

Charlie was already different from other children.

He was used to not being able run very far and having such a loud cough that people looked at him funnily.

He didn't want them to think that he was now mad too.

Charlie could only imagine how the conversation might go.

"Hey mum and dad. Do you remember that little lightning strike that nearly killed me and put me in hospital the other day?

"Well, it appears to have left me with a floating target in front of my eyes."

That was a conversation that Charlie did not

intend on having with anyone at the moment.

He was convinced the strange shape would disappear after he had fully rested and was back to his old self.

Tucked up on the couch with a duvet and a stack of DVDs, Charlie settled into a dull week of resting, reading, watching TV and generally being bored at home.

Looking out of his lounge window he knew the rest of his pals were concentrating on the real goal: being in top shape for the long-awaited Hall Park trials.

And he would just have to be patient.

6. WAITING GAME

The days dragged by.

The following weekend Joe came round to see Charlie along with Peter, one of their best friends.

Peter was almost as small as Charlie but, unlike his pal, had no problem in running.

In fact, he was like lightning around the football pitch.

He always played as a tricky winger but had been injured for the past two months.

Somehow he had managed to fall out of a treehouse in the back garden of his cousin's house, breaking his left leg in the fall.

The fall had been only about six feet but it was enough to break the bone in two places.

Peter had been in plaster and then on crutches, forced to miss the end-of-season title run-in – a massive blow for Blackfriars.

And he would not be able to take part in the Hall Park trials either.

His left leg was not strong enough yet to play sport again.

It was just one of those unlucky things.

Not that you would know from Peter.

He wasn't upset or angry, which was typical of his easy-going attitude.

He simply shrugged his shoulders and laughed it off.

"There will be plenty of other opportunities," he told Joe and Charlie shortly after the accident.

Now it was Charlie they were trying to cheer up.

They had called in to see their injured friend on their way to the Rec.

Peter was going to throw the ball for Joe to practice his catching.

As usual, they were both wearing their United shirts.

Charlie was a blue and sighed when he saw the red tops wander through his door.

Football rivalries aside though, he was chuffed to see them both. A week inside his house had seemed like a lifetime.

There was only so many video games and films that Charlie could stomach without looking out of the window into the early summer sunshine.

"You'll still make the trials. There's plenty of time yet," said Peter, casually flicking through a football magazine on Charlie's bed.

"Yes, he's right Charlie. There's loads of time to make the trial," Joe agreed, pushing his long brown hair out of his eyes.

Charlie nodded glumly.

He played with the drawstring on his black hoodie awkwardly, not knowing what to say.

He hated the fact they were going to the Rec without him – even if Peter was still unable to properly kick a ball.

A wicked smile flashed across Joe's face.

"So, you even managed to miss the lightning bolt? Just about sums up your football career so far, doesn't it Fry?"

The two boys chuckled and even Charlie forced a half-smile, aware the leg-pulling would have to begin at some point.

"So what happened then?"

"I'm not sure. I left you and was heading home quickly because of the rain.

"Then Mum rang me and I answered. We had a really quick chat and then I was trying to put my phone away and... bang! The next thing I knew I was in hospital."

Peter blew out his cheeks.

"Wow. You are one lucky guy.

"You were that close to a bolt of lightning and you survived? It's pretty amazing when you think about it."

Charlie didn't feel like he was lucky.

He had spent hours thinking about missing that sitter at the end of the North Street game.

How had he missed it?

Had he closed his eyes at the wrong moment?

Even now, Charlie could feel the ball connecting his outstretched foot rather than rolling past.

He had played his small – but match-changing – role in the game over and over in his mind, thinking about what he could have done differently.

It was keeping him awake at night – but it was not the only thing weighing on his mind.

Even as Peter spoke, the mystery floating shape kept cutting across Charlie's eyesight as he looked at his friends.

He said nothing to them but it was beginning to freak him out. He closed his eyes and changed the subject.

"Yeah, I guess. How's school?"

Peter and Joe looked at each other, neither replying immediately.

"What is it?" said Charlie, sensing something was wrong.

Joe shrugged. "That moron Adam keeps making threats against us."

Charlie tensed. "What has he been saying?"

"The usual nonsense – he'll break my hands before the trial. You know the kind of thing," Joe replied.

Charlie nodded but his stomach was in knots.

He knew Adam would never dare to threaten Joe. He was too big, too confident, too much trouble for the gang to deal with.

Deep down, he knew the threats were being made about him and his role in the league defeat – and his friends were trying to protect him.

This didn't sound good.

Joe gave him a playful tap on the shoulder.

"Don't worry about it. They're idiots but school is nearly over.

"We'll be off to secondary school in September and we'll never have to see those morons again – unless we're all selected to play for Hall Park, of course."

Charlie snorted at Joe's optimism.

He could feel the butterflies churning in his stomach.

School on Monday would not be fun.

7. BACK TO SCHOOL

Despite Charlie's nerves, school was not too bad.

Most of his classmates had been sympathetic, showing real kindness towards him.

Almost everyone wanted to talk about the lightning bolt, temporarily promoting Charlie to a mini celebrity.

Much to Joe and Peter's amusement, Charlie had a gang of younger kids following him around wanting to talk about the 'miracle' that had happened to him.

At first, he was shy but Charlie soon became used to the regular barrage of questions and high-fives.

Secretly he enjoyed the all of the fuss; being the centre of attention made a nice change.

And, being surrounded by a crowd all the time meant that Adam, Seamus and Lee could never get too close to him.

Charlie couldn't miss the gang scowling at him, childishly whispering behind their hands and staring in his direction before laughing menacingly.

But they couldn't touch him, despite a few whispered threats on the first day.

Joe or Peter was never too far away anyway and the hospital had insisted Charlie remained inside at break time rather than going outside with the others.

The doctors did not want to risk Charlie's health by putting him straight back into the rough and tumble of the playground.

He couldn't practice football but in private Charlie was relieved. It gave the bullies no chance to target him.

He felt ashamed to feel so scared, a secret he kept to himself.

He knew what his dad would say: "Be brave. You've got to face up to your problems."

It was not that easy though.

For starters, Charlie certainly didn't feel brave.

He was a lot smaller than all of them and he hated fighting.

Trying to talk to those goons would have been completely pointless so there was only ever going to be one winner – and it wouldn't be him.

They made him sick with their sneering and mocking.

No-one felt worse about what happened at the football match than him, why couldn't they see that?

Charlie was desperately trying to put the last game out of his mind.

He needed to focus on the upcoming Hall Park trials and not dwell on what went woefully wrong last week.

Predictably after a few days, Charlie's new-found fame began to wear off as the other kids lost interest.

There were only so many questions they could ask

and listen to the same story over and over again.

By Friday, things were almost back to normal. Break and lunchtimes were spent with Peter and Joe, usually talking football and the Hall Park trial.

Joe had arranged to go to the Rec on Saturday morning to give Charlie his first run out.

Peter was swimming in the morning – as part of his recovery – but was planning to meet up with them in the afternoon.

"Looking forward to getting back out on the pitch, star striker?" Joe asked as he grabbed Charlie in a playful headlock, confident his best mate had now recovered from the lightning ordeal.

"Get off." Charlie pushed him away and tried to straighten his T-shirt.

"Don't call me that … but yes, I can't wait to play again.

"How do professional footballers cope with being injured for months?

"They must go stir crazy!"

Peter laughed.

He was always jovial and never seemed down.

Charlie admired his ability to always find the good in anything or anybody.

He replied: "Well, you're not on the sick list any longer, Fry!

"Wait for tomorrow, you'll be sick of the Rec. We've already planned it.

"Football with Joe in the morning then we're doing running once I bowl up in the afternoon. It's going to be a proper workout."

Charlie shrugged. "You know I can't run far..."

Joe cut in: "If you're a striker, you don't need to run for miles.

"You're not playing in midfield!

"You just need to be smart about when you run, and be quick when you do it."

Charlie looked at both of his friends with confusion on his face.

"How do you both know that I'm planning to try out as a striker?"

Joe and Peter looked at each other and began laughing.

Smiling kindly, Joe said: "Charlie Fry, you've waited for your whole life for this trial.

"You've always been the striker whenever we've played down the park.

"You were never going to the trial for any of the other positions!"

Peter chipped in: "And what rubbish friends we'd be if we didn't know that!

"Don't worry Fry-inho, you'll be fighting fit for the big day."

Charlie grinned at Peter using his Brazilian nickname – something he'd adopted after watching the Samba stars at the last World Cup.

"Thanks guys."

He had the best friends in the world and he would not let them down.

Slapping them both on the back, Charlie and his friends headed back towards their classroom for the final lesson of the day.

None of them saw Adam lurking silently in a nearby doorway, listening intently to every word they said.

8. THE GIFT

It was a bright and sunny morning.

Charlie had been first up in the Fry household.

He had bolted down his breakfast, finished his medication and been out of the door before his dad had even got out of the shower.

His time had come.

He arrived at the Rec 20 minutes before he was supposed to meet with Joe, bouncing his leather ball as he marched along the path heading towards the line of trees.

They always practiced in the same spot – and had been doing it for years. It was like a second home to them.

The Rec was almost deserted this early in the morning with most people still eating breakfast or lazing around in bed.

It meant their goalmouth was not taken up by anyone else.

Two healthy tree trunks provided sturdy goalposts, the grass worn away from Joe's dives and kicking.

In the winter it could be a mud-bath but it was the

perfect size for them to practice.

Of course, they would have loved proper goals but Manor Park was the only place with goalposts up all year round – and that was right across the other side of town.

Charlie, Joe and Peter were happy with their little patch of turf, spending years on that makeshift pitch.

Sometimes more boys turned up and they had a proper match.

At other times it was just the three of them, practicing the soccer skills that they hoped would lead to a professional career in the future.

Charlie threw his water bottle down and took off his black hoodie.

He was wearing his Blues shirt and long, baggy shorts.

He'd opted for his trainers rather than his boots – he still hadn't cleaned them since the game against North Street.

They were a grim sight but Charlie hadn't had time this morning.

He'd clean them one evening in the week, he had promised himself.

There was still a slight chill in the air and the grass was wet with dew but Charlie could already tell it was going to be a warm day.

He left the ball in the centre of the goal.

Despite summer's early arrival, the goalmouth was still soft and muddy – Joe would be pleased.

Charlie knew that Joe's mum, who washed her son's muddy goalkeeper kits almost every day, would not be so thrilled.

Charlie began a light jog and knew straight away that he was totally out of shape.

Two weeks of resting now made exercising so much harder.

His breathing quickened only a few seconds after he began to move.

Charlie ran for about 20 metres before he was completely out of breath, reaching for the trusty inhaler in his pocket.

He spluttered as he desperately tried to get more air into his lungs and doubled over as if he'd run a full marathon.

That stupid lightning bolt still had an awful lot to answer for.

Charlie began to panic, sensing that familiar feeling of nervousness creep up inside his chest.

The trials were a week away and he could run even less than normal.

How could he take part in the trials if he couldn't run at all?

Deep in thought, Charlie slouched back to the ball in the goalmouth.

Walking slowly, he had been able to regain his breath.

But he was angry – really angry.

He did not have time to get up to full fitness before the trial.

Would he even be able to take part next Saturday?

And even if he did, how could he manage to impress the Hall Park coaches if he could barely run?

Unable to control his temper any longer, Charlie lashed out – smashing the ball against a nearby tree in fury.

He swung his right leg with all his might, furious his chances of getting into Hall Park's team were getting less every second.

And then it happened.
Bang!
Charlie's life changed forever.

9. TARGET PRACTICE

The ball flew into the tree trunk and rebounded straight into Charlie's stomach with such force that it knocked him over.

Dazed and surprised, Charlie scratched his head as he found himself lying flat out on the grass looking towards the sky.

He looked around to see if anyone else had witnessed the bizarre incident happen.

Thankfully, no-one seemed to have watched Charlie managing to knock himself over with a football.

He was almost alone in the park apart from a handful of dogs and their owners.

None of them were anywhere near him and all seemed to have completely missed his moment of embarrassment.

Feeling foolish and blushing, he slowly stood up from the wet grass, brushing the water off his beloved shirt.

He was glad Joe and Peter hadn't arrived in time to see his comedy act.

But what had happened?

The strange floating shape in his eyesight was behind this, Charlie knew.

Even so, Charlie looked suspiciously at the ball, which was sitting still a couple of metres away from him.

He tried to recount exactly what had happened. As he had lashed out at the ball, the target seemed to zoom onto the tree.

It was usually black but as soon as it fixed on the tree trunk, it had flashed green.

Charlie tried to focus on the target now.

There it was – swirling pointlessly in front of his eyes as usual. It was now black again, harmlessly floating around his vision.

Although it was odd, Charlie had almost become used to seeing it but this was the first time it had changed colour or moved so quickly.

It seemed to be a targeting system, like the kind used on some video games.

Charlie shook his head at such a crazy thought. Nonetheless, he picked the ball up and placed it five metres away from the tree.

His eyes locked on the ball, concentrating on kicking as hard as he could.

The mystery shape did nothing, casually floating around his eyesight like normal. No sign of it turning green.

Charlie closed his eyes, hoping it would make the target burst into life.

It didn't.

Confused, the footballer stood and looked at the ball, not moving a muscle.

He realised he must have looked really daft if anyone else was watching him but he did not care.

He simply had to work this puzzle out.

The mystery shape remained drifting around his vision.

He took a step towards the ball – and everything changed.

As soon as he moved, the target leapt into the centre of his vision.

Surprised by the sudden movement Charlie forgot to look at the tree, his full concentration on the target in front of him.

The target stopped flashing and turned green a split second before his right foot connected with the leather football.

Charlie did not kick the ball too hard this time but, if he was worried about the ball rebounding off the tree, he did not need to.

It ran along the floor, straight ahead of him and missing the tree trunk by about two metres.

However it went exactly where the target had been planted in his eyesight only a second before.

Charlie was confused, scratching his short brown hair as he pondered the situation.

The target had now returned to its normal state, floating innocently around his eyesight.

It was almost as if the target only came to life as Charlie went to kick the ball.

Not only that, that target looked familiar – Charlie had seen it somewhere before but he couldn't remember where.

It was beginning to bug him.

Charlie closed his eyes and attempted to run through what had happened, trying to understand this strange new power he'd stumbled upon.

After a minute of thought, he moved back to the ball to try again.

He looked at the ball trying to work out how many paces he would need to make before making contact.

Then he looked up, focusing completely on the tree trunk.

He was guessing the target would fix upon wherever his gaze directed it.

The shape was still floating aimlessly around his vision and did not move to the tree.

But once again that changed as soon as he began moving to kick the ball.

The shape flashed green and zoomed straight onto the tree trunk – the exact spot Charlie had focused upon.

Wary after last time, Charlie side-footed the ball towards the tree and backed away.

He watched it trickle along the floor and hit the middle of the trunk about a metre underneath his target.

The ball bounced away harmlessly as Charlie scratched his chin, seeking answers about his new power.

He was confused: the target seemed to only work when Charlie was moving to kick the ball – turning green and locking onto the exact spot he was aiming for.

But the target didn't generate any power, Charlie realised.

It directed the ball but the force of the shot had to come from him, otherwise the ball would just trickle along the floor like his last attempt.

And most importantly, when the target went green, it looked familiar to him. Where had he seen it before?

Charlie's thoughts were interrupted by the sound of footsteps approaching behind him.

"Joe, I've got something to tell you," Charlie said as he turned around expecting to see his good friend approaching.

The punch went straight into Charlie's stomach, sending him crashing to the ground and knocking all the air out of him.

Charlie gasped for air as Adam stood above him. Lee and Seamus stood a couple of yards back sniggering.

"Nope, it's only us. It's payback time, Fry."

10. BULLIES

Charlie lay crumpled on the wet grass, desperately trying to regain his breath.

"I warned you, Fry, about playing football again, didn't I?

"Your pathetic lightning bolt story may have bought you some sympathy from the teachers, parents and the school muppets but we've not forgotten how you cost us the league.

"We've been waiting for you – and now you're going to pay."

Ignoring the searing pain in his stomach, Charlie glanced up at Adam. His bright blue eyes were full of menace, he looked quite crazy with his shaved head.

Charlie wanted to speak, to explain what had happened but no words came out.

He was properly winded and felt like he was going to be sick.

"LEAVE HIM ALONE!"

Out of nowhere Joe charged into Adam, knocking him over.

As he turned to face them, Seamus and Lee both

jumped on Joe's back, wrestling him to the floor.

The three of them sprawled across the grass, wrestling each other frantically to try and get the upper hand.

Despite two of them trying to pin him down, Joe's size meant he was easily strong enough to match the pair of them.

But Adam jumped back to his feet and piled on top of Joe's back, allowing his cronies to grab and arm each and pin Joe down.

"Nice try, hero," Adam sneered. "Shame you turned up so late – otherwise you might have been able to save your sad little friend."

Joe wrestled against the boys' grips but this time could not shake them off.

The three of them stood up awkwardly, several feet away from Adam.

Brushing his hands together, he moved back towards Charlie, who was now on his hands and knees still struggling for breath.

"Do NOT touch him! If you do, I'll make you pay, I swear."

Joe's cheeks were red and his face looked like thunder.

Charlie had seen Joe annoyed before but never this upset. He looked scary.

Adam hesitated at Joe's words – a threat from the big keeper could not be taken lightly.

He grinned, a smile full of spite.

"Go for it and try your best. Perhaps it's you who should be worried – you're next on our list after this little weasel."

Seamus and Lee laughed at Adam's insult.

Satisfied he had put Joe in his place, Adam turned

towards Charlie and kicked him hard in the stomach.

Charlie collapsed again, curling into a little ball on the ground for protection.

He could not breathe from the nasty kick in the ribs. He felt lightheaded through a lack of oxygen.

Adam began to laugh – a cruel, horrible sound above Charlie's head.

"Look, boys... oomph," Adam stopped in mid-sentence as Peter rugby tackled him from behind sending him sprawling to the floor

Shocked at Peter's unexpected entrance, Seamus and Lee made the mistake of loosening their grip on Joe for a second.

It was all he needed.

As soon as their hands slightly relaxed, Joe sprang.

He knocked Seamus over before turning to Lee, who ran away without the protection of his bigger friends.

Joe grabbed Adam as he struggled back to his feet. Holding him up with a bear-like paw fixed around the bully's throat, Joe spoke calmly and quietly.

"Never come near us again, Knight – you or your cowardly mates. Do you understand me?"

Now outnumbered and outmuscled, Adam had lost his cockiness.

He nodded his head the tiniest fraction, looking at the floor and avoiding eye contact.

Charlie noticed he was holding his shoulder where Peter had charged straight into him.

"Now, go away and don't come back."

Joe roughly flung Adam in the direction of Seamus who had retreated several metres away and was looking at Peter and Joe warily.

Seamus muttered: "Come on, Ad," and turned to

leave.

Adam waited a little longer before departing, disgustingly spitting on the floor in Joe's direction before following his friends.

Joe and Peter eyeballed the gang as they left the park, all three slouching away towards the exit to lick their wounds.

They noticed a stranger on a bike seemed to have been watching the fight from a long distance away.

The person was too far away to be recognised though and soon departed too.

Apart from the mystery biker, their part of the park was still virtually deserted.

Joe turned to Peter and slapped him on the back. "You arrived in the nick of time, old boy!"

Peter grinned and shrugged.

"You looked like you had it under control. I just couldn't resist giving Knight a taste of the mud though."

Joe looked sideways at Peter.

He may not have been tall but he was stocky and had plenty of guts. In short, he was a pretty tough cookie.

"Thanks guys."

They turned around to find Charlie back on his feet but looking like he'd been involved in a boxing match.

They helped him towards a nearby bench and the three of them sat down in the early morning sunshine, swigging from their water bottles.

Some deep breathing and a couple of puffs from his inhaler saw Charlie recover quickly.

He was soon back to his usual self but decided to keep the target mystery to himself.

If he didn't understand it for himself, how could he even begin to explain it to the others?

Instead he listened to his friends' animated discussion over the fight and whether Adam and the gang would come looking for them again.

"They're just morons," Joe said, leaning back on the bench and looking back towards the park's exit where the gang had left.

Peter nodded in agreement: "Yeah, they wanted to get Charlie on his own rather than face all three of us. What a bunch of cowards."

"Will they ever leave me alone?" Charlie asked, knowing the answer already.

They were not the type of forgive and forget.

Joe playfully punched him on the arm. "You won't need to worry about them when you're knocking the goals in for Hall Park!

"Come on, let's get practicing!"

Joe jumped up from the bench but then paused as another thought dawned on him.

"Wait, Pete, I thought you weren't turning up until later? What are you doing here?"

Charlie turned towards Peter too.

"Yeah, I thought that too…. although I'm very glad you turned up when you did!" he added quickly.

Peter shot them both a wicked smile. "I've been waiting for you to ask.

"You're both right, I was due to go swimming this morning.

"But my dad spoke to the hospital consultant last night and they've given me the all clear. I can play football again and that means…"

With a feeling of excitement growing in his stomach, Charlie interrupted: "… you're going to try out for Hall Park?"

Peter nodded.

"Yes. Charlie, you'll need another centre-forward alongside you – me. We'll score a bucket load of goals, you wait and see."

Charlie could not help but smile.

As the friends whooped and cheered their way back towards the makeshift goal, he was happier than he'd been in a very, very long time.

11. STRIKER

"Fry! You're on fire!"

Joe had been beaten for about the hundredth time.

Peter had left the Rec a couple of hours ago, exhausted after being injured for so long.

Charlie and Joe had stayed – practicing headers, one-on-ones, penalties and crosses as well as some running too.

It was teatime and they were nearly finished.

Adam and the bullies had not reappeared since the fight leaving the boys to concentrate fully on football.

Charlie was still trying to master using the target but he was getting better.

He had not told Joe or Peter about his new-found ability – but his friends had been surprised at Charlie's improved shooting skills.

By now, Charlie had almost mastered the art of being able to choose a spot, fix the target and watch it fly straight into the selected location.

He was beginning to understand the gift – and could feel the excitement growing in his tummy.

This was something special.

As far as Charlie could tell, as soon as the target had flashed green and locked into place, the ball would directly head towards that particular spot.

Once he'd selected the target, Charlie just had to add the power.

If he selected the top corner, he had to kick the ball hard.

But if he wanted to carefully roll the ball into the bottom corner of the goal, a more gentle kick was needed.

Charlie was smart though.

He realised that, as he could apparently no longer miss (as long as he managed to get the target working properly), his best chance of scoring would be to smash the ball as hard as his legs would allow – every single time.

But people would surely become suspicious. No one scored every single shot they took, especially not an 11-year-old.

Joe had been scratching his head after Charlie scored ten penalties in a row without missing a single one.

It wasn't normal.

Seeing Joe's confusion at his outstanding performance from the penalty spot, it dawned on Charlie that he needed to be unpredictable.

So he had begun to mix it up.

Sometimes he would hit the ball straight at Joe, other chances he would put deliberately wide.

On occasion he would put the target within Joe's reach and hit the ball softly enough for the 'keeper to get a glove on his shot and make the save.

All day he practiced using the target and was now able to flick it towards a chosen spot in a split second.

Whether the ball went wide of the goal, was saved or screamed into the top corner did not matter.

What was important was the ball went where he told it to.

And it was working.

Free-kicks, penalties, volleys and long shots peppered Joe's goal – all from Charlie's wand of a right boot.

Headers and running with the ball had proved more difficult though, particularly when one-on-one with Joe.

Charlie realised that concentrating on the ball, Joe rushing out of his goal and getting the target in place was proving difficult.

It was a lot to deal with in a short space of time.

He told himself he needed to practice moving with the ball later in the week as he sent yet another curler into the top corner, leaving Joe grasping thin air once more.

Brimming with enthusiasm, Charlie bounced between the goalposts eager to retrieve the ball and attempt yet another long range effort.

But when he turned around, it was clear that Joe was finished for the day. Covered in mud, his buddy was still on his hands and knees.

He looked exhausted. Charlie jogged over and helped his friend to his feet.

Although Charlie was disappointed to finally stop, he knew he had not played football for weeks and guessed his legs would ache in the morning.

Excitement was the only thing that had kept him going for so long.

But Joe, who was one of the most loyal people you could meet, did not have the same adrenaline going through his body.

He had stayed for hours to help Charlie practice, unwilling to let his friend down.

Joe had big bags under his steel-blue eyes, his square jaw covered in mud.

He took a long swig of his almost-empty water bottle as Charlie spoke.

"Shall we call it a day, Joe?

"Thanks for all the help. I feel much fitter already. It's been such a good day."

Joe turned to look at his friend, who seemed have turned into some sort of footballing superstar overnight.

He could not remember being beaten so many times, despite making plenty of saves later in the afternoon.

His body ached from all the diving around.

"Have you been practicing in your back garden, Fry-inho?

"Or have I lost my touch?"

Charlie swallowed, feeling a little guilty.

He had not given a thought about Joe or considered if smashing the ball past his friend repeatedly would dent his confidence – a quality needed for all good goalkeepers.

He spoke slowly so Joe would know he was being serious.

"Don't be daft. You are the best goalkeeper in this town and probably the county.

"I know it. You know it.

"I bet Hall Park have already got you penned down for their team – even before the trials.

"I had a good day today, mainly because of the advice and tips my friends have given me."

Joe stared back at him for a moment and broke into a grin.

"I hope you're right, Boy Wonder!

"And, if you keep up this kind of form, Fry, then we'll both be playing for HP Rovers next season."

The goalie grabbed his friend in a gentle headlock and together they began wandering home for tea, leaving the muddy makeshift goalmouth behind them.

12. THE APP MYSTERY

Charlie had been right. His entire body was sore the next day.

After his time in hospital and resting at home following the lightning bolt accident, he'd lost some of his fitness.

Disappointed but determined not to pick up an injury at such a vital time, he rang Joe and told him that he could not play that day.

But he insisted that he'd be back on the Rec tomorrow night after school.

Still it gave him the chance to practice in private, putting the finishes touches to the skills he had spent perfecting the day before.

He spent the day in his back garden, convincing Harry to try and play as the 'keeper.

Harry was six and did not really like football.

But he happily pulled on the gloves – anything to have his big brother's full attention for an afternoon.

Charlie instructed Harry to run towards him at full speed, trying to stop the ball if he could.

The Fry back garden was narrow and long so

Charlie would have a couple of seconds before Harry reached the ball – but there would not be too much room either side of his little brother to slot the ball into the goal.

It was a challenge and absolutely perfect.

Time and time again, Harry rushed out.

At times he was screaming so loudly that their mum had to tell them to quieten down out of the kitchen window.

And despite his best efforts, Charlie still could not manage to direct the ball in time.

Eventually he opted for a simple technique.

As soon as he started running, he picked his spot and locked the target in place.

Then he concentrated on the goalkeeper, picking different times to slot the ball past Harry whenever the targeted area was exposed.

It worked a treat.

He scored six in row before Harry saved one and then another eight in a row.

Harry got fed up eventually, annoyed the ball kept going past him.

To stop him from going inside to play something else, Charlie convinced his little brother to throw the ball so he could practice headers.

Thirty minutes later, Charlie had got to grips with heading using the target too.

He was all set.

He would only have another couple of practice sessions at the Rec before the big trial but Charlie had never been so confident.

He could score goals as long as he got the chance.

His dad called him into the house, reminding him it was time for physiotherapy.

Taking a puff on his inhaler to regain his breath, Charlie ruffled Harry's hair as a thank you.

The young boy looked chuffed that his big brother had played with him for so long.

He ran inside, shouting: "Mum, mum! Charlie is sick at football!"

Charlie watched Harry disappear into the living room before reluctantly dragging himself upstairs towards his bedroom to begin his daily physio session.

He stopped at the doorway, noticing a strange object on his bed.

A new smart phone was sitting on his pillow.

Charlie stood open mouthed, gawping at the latest technology that appeared to be his.

His dad appeared behind him, speaking softly.

"You didn't think I would forget, did you?"

Charlie did not say a word.

He simply turned and hugged his dad tightly. He was the best.

The pair spent the next few minutes looking at the phone's latest features, discussing the improvements made to it.

Charlie and his dad shared a passion for technology.

After ten minutes, his dad left and Charlie began the process of installing his old data and apps as he started his daily breathing activities.

He flicked open his favourite flick football app to check his high score had been transferred over too.

Then he realised: he finally knew where the target embedded in his vision had come from.

How had he not realised before?

The mystery object was also floating on his

phone's screen – it was part of a game on an app.

Charlie's mind began racing, his heart thumping. How could this even be possible?

13. PROVE IT

"You have got to be kidding," said Joe, looking confused.

Peter, Joe and Charlie were sitting in their goalmouth at the Rec.

The big Hall Park trial would take place on Saturday, in less than 48 hours' time.

It was nearing 8.30pm and they were almost the last ones to leave the park.

They had been playing for almost two hours – and Charlie had been unstoppable.

His back garden training with Harry throughout the week had made him sharp, able to place the target in a split second.

His right boot did the rest. Or his left – it didn't matter anymore.

There could be little doubt: Charlie Fry was a goal machine.

He was still shorter than everyone else, much smaller and could not run very far, but if he got a clear sight of goal, there would only be one outcome.

Seeing his friends' looks of surprise – not to

mention a little suspicion – convinced Charlie to tell them his big secret.

Now they looked stunned instead.

Joe shook his head.

"I'm sorry, Charlie. I'm really struggling to believe this."

Peter had been staring intently at the ground as Charlie spoke.

Upon hearing Joe's doubts, he spoke up: "Charlie, let me get this straight.

"You get struck by lightning while you're holding your phone.

"Somehow the lightning bolt transfers the football target inside your favourite app into your brain.

"The target is there all the time but only comes to life when you play football.

"And when you place the target – this one inside your head that we can't see – the ball always goes in that spot?"

Charlie nodded, realising how crazy it sounded when said out loud.

Still he had shared everything with Peter and Joe for as long as he could remember – they had to believe him now.

He couldn't do this without them.

Joe snorted. "This is rubbish. I don't know what's wrong with you, Charlie, but this is the biggest load of nonsense I've ever heard.

"I've not got the time to listen this … fairy tale."

And with those damning words, Charlie's best friend turned his back and began heading towards the gate.

"Wait, Joe, let me explain…" Charlie began but his words were not answered.

Charlie could only watch as Joe left the park without turning back once.

He turned to Peter, who was chewing his lip thoughtfully.

Finally he looked at Charlie again: "Okay, Fry. Prove it."

Peter jogged over to his bike, lying on the grass behind the trees that acted as goalposts.

He wheeled it twenty metres away and placed it down on the turf, picking up his backpack as well as the friends' water bottles as he returned to the goalmouth.

He spaced out the three objects – each about five metres apart – and turned back to Charlie, who was looking a tad confused.

Standing behind the bottle positioned furthest to Charlie's left, Peter dug out an old tennis ball wedged into his shorts pocket.

"Okay, Mr Magic.

"Let's see what you're made of. You stand over by my bike.

"I'll throw this tennis ball up into the air. You volley it and knock over the target I'm standing behind.

"If this target ... thing ... is real, then this should be a piece of cake."

Charlie shrugged but began walking towards the bike nonetheless.

It was a simple challenge – but at least Peter was willing to give him a chance. It was far more than Joe had done.

Joe had always been there for Charlie.

It made him feel sick to think his friend could not even bear to look at him now.

He took a deep breath, facing Peter who was standing several feet behind the first water bottle prepared to retrieve the ball after Charlie's attempted volley.

"Ready?" Peter held the ball in his right hand, waiting for Charlie to start.

Charlie looked around.

It was nearly dark so the sun wouldn't get in his eyes.

It was strange.

He knew he could do it but this was the first time someone expected him to do it.

He was being tested to perform under pressure.

It wasn't a nice feeling but Charlie swallowed determinedly and tried to focus.

"Yes."

Peter threw the ball high into the air. Charlie watched it carefully, moving to his left.

As the ball began to fall, Charlie's eyes flicked onto the water bottle in front of Peter.

The target snapped onto the bottle and turned green in a flash.

Immediately Charlie's eyes flew back to the ball – his right foot meeting it sweetly about half a metre above the ground.

The timing was perfect.

As soon as it left Charlie's trainer, the ball flew flat over the ground before knocking the water bottle over.

Peter watched the empty bottle cartwheel away over the floor, bouncing in the opposite direction to the tennis ball.

He hurried to retrieve the ball, saying nothing but raising his eyebrows in appreciation at Charlie's first attempt.

The young lad moved behind the next water bottle and waited for Charlie to give the signal that he was ready.

Thirty seconds later, the water bottle was also spinning away and Peter was chasing after the ball once more.

The third and final target was Peter's backpack.

Charlie knew he couldn't knock that over with a tennis ball so he opted for a new approach – giving Peter a small taste of his soccer skills.

As the ball went up into the air, Charlie locked onto the backpack with the targeting system.

It all came so naturally to him now, it was done in the blink of an eye.

But instead of volleying the ball with full power, Charlie opted to meet it this time with a controlled side-footed effort.

The ball left Charlie's foot, looped up and gently dropped on top of the backpack and nestled on top of the target.

Charlie blew out his cheeks out with a sigh of relief.

He had done it.

The Boy Wonder looked at Peter with concern, crossing his fingers and silently praying that he would not react like Joe had earlier.

Peter walked up to the backpack, gazing at the tennis ball now sitting upon it.

He gazed back at Charlie, his face breaking into a huge grin as he walked towards him.

"Charlie Fry.

"Whether you can see imaginary targets or not, you are totally awesome at football."

Peter draped a friendly arm around his mate as he spoke.

"And that is enough for me.

"Roll on the weekend!

"We are going to score a hatful of goals in front of the Hall Park scouts on Saturday."

14. A NASTY SURPRISE

Almost everybody in Crickledon turned out for the annual Hall Park trials.

Along with the summer carnival and the annual bonfire night, it was one of the main events in the town's social calendar.

There were so many boys wanting to get into the Hall Park training squad, four matches were played at the same time on the Hall Park training pitches.

Club scouts and coaches watched each of the games, carefully casting expert eyes over the players in each contest.

The lucky few who were selected were told the good news in the following week – and invited to the Hall Park summer training camp in Skegness.

Big dark circles under Charlie's eyes revealed he had not had much sleep.

All his footballing dreams rested on today.

His new gift had given him some much-needed

confidence but he was still worried. It was part of his character.

What if the coaches thought he was lazy because he hardly ran?

Would this be a repeat of the North Street game all over again?

And would his new power actually work in a match?

His dad drove to the trials, picking up Peter on the way.

Peter's dad was a plumber and had been called out on an emergency but would meet them later at the game.

Everyone talked excitedly on the journey, knowing this was a day to savour.

Throughout the trip both Charlie's parents repeatedly insisted football was only a game – and not life and death.

Charlie took no notice. He knew they were trying to help but he was struggling badly with nerves. He felt the familiar sick feeling in his stomach again.

His dad parked on the grass verge outside Hall Park's ramshackle old stadium alongside hundreds of other vehicles.

The boys jumped out of the car and ran ahead, looking for Pitch Three where their trial was due to take place in less than 30 minutes.

Breathless from the sprint, Charlie followed Peter towards the training pitch near a set of large conifer trees. A large group of lads were already gathered round.

Charlie knew most of the faces in the group.

Joe stood in the middle, talking intently to a man who Charlie guessed was one of Hall Park's coaches.

They had not spoken since the row at the Rec the other night. It was the longest that they had ever fallen out for.

As the pair approached, Joe looked up gave his friends a small nod and wandered off towards some players warming up.

The white-haired coach looked fed up already, holding a clipboard tightly in his right hand and a pen in the other.

He looked briefly at Charlie and Peter before barking out his words.

"Names?"

"Charlie Fry."

"Peter Bell."

The coach scanned the list in front of him. "Yes, you're on the list – and you're both in my Blue team.

"Grab a bib, put your boots on and join the others over there."

He nodded in the direction of several other small lads, trying unsuccessfully to pass the ball between themselves.

"Oh, and here's the team-sheet."

Eager to move onto the next group, he did not wait for a reply before thrusting the piece of paper into Peter's hands and marching off.

Charlie looked over at Joe again.

He was talking with Adam, Seamus and Lee – apparently deep in a tense conversation.

A few feet away from them stood another group; Bishop, Peppermint and several others of the North Street team.

"Oh no."

Charlie turned back to see Peter's face crinkled up with worry. Peter rarely looked angry or concerned so something must be badly wrong.

"What's wrong?"

"These teams are stupid. They're fixed.

"It's like they've already decided who the best players are and put them all into one team. We've got to play against them."

Charlie couldn't believe the trial would be so unfair.

How could he score goals if his team never had the ball?

But then he saw exactly what had upset Peter so much.

Joe was playing on the other team.

15. U-TURN

Charlie and Peter looked at each other and began putting on their boots without saying another word.

What more could be said?

Their team were absolute no-hopers and their chances of making the Hall Park training squad was more unlikely than ever.

And to top it all off, they would be facing their best mate – not to mention by far the best goalkeeper in the town – too.

The silence was broken by a familiar voice, oozing malice as usual: "So the reserves have finally turned up at last?"

Adam had dawdled across the pitch, accompanied by Seamus and Lee. Joe was now nowhere to be seen.

With a little chuckle, Adam continued: "Bet you didn't know that Seamus' old man is a Hall Park coach?

"We spent last night letting him know all about the talented players – and who the time-wasters were.

"It seems like he listened to us and has managed to put all our recommendations into his Red team, leaving you chumps with useless old Barney Williams as coach.

"That's real bad luck for you boys, isn't it?

"Even your best mate made it into the Red team, or the 'A' team as some people may call it.

Pity you didn't, Fry. Ready for a good thrashing today?"

Upset at the unfairness of the situation, Charlie sprang to his feet. "Do one, Knight. I can't be bothered to listen to your rubbish this morning."

Shocked at Charlie's unexpectedly aggressive response, Adam leaned in closer and snarled: "Careful, Fry.

"If you don't mind your manners, you and your little girlfriend here might be leaving in an ambulance rather than with Mummy and Daddy."

Peter stepped between them and pushed Adam away, mocking him: "Try it then, Big Man. Go on!"

Barney heard the commotion, looked over and began heading towards the group.

Adam retreated several steps, heading back towards his team on the other side of the pitch. Seamus and Lee had already made a sharp exit.

He pointed at Peter and whispered. "I'll see you out there."

The bully turned and ran straight into Joe, who had crept up silently to stand directly behind him.

"You speak to my mates like that again, Knight, and we'll be having words. Is that clear?"

Adam shrunk under Joe's fierce glare.

He stepped back a few paces and began to circle away from the burly keeper.

"You had better remember whose side you're on now, Foster. You'll be ending these losers' football dreams in a few minutes."

Joe stepped towards Charlie and Peter, turning his back on Adam.

"No, I won't.

"I've asked Barney to play for his team and he's agreed.

"I'd rather lose with these guys than win with you. Now go away."

Open-mouthed, Adam stood stock still for a moment before slouching off to join Seamus and Lee.

Joe looked at Charlie.

"I'm sorry I behaved like a prat. I should have believed you."

Peter smiled.

"Have you really switched teams or are you just winding Mr Angry Man up?"

Joe shrugged: "What's the point in being a goalkeeper if there's nothing to do?

"Much better to be busy and make some saves rather than barely touch the ball.

"And besides, a little bird told me that Barney's team has a couple of tricky strikers up their sleeve so I didn't fancy facing them too much."

Joe grinned and stuck out his hand to Charlie, who grabbed it eagerly.

Win or lose, they would be playing in the Hall Park trials together.

16. SKIPPER

Barney's pre-match team talk was confusing.

It made little sense. He seemed to want to play possession football but with six defenders on the pitch.

He called everyone by their hair colour, meaning there were six "blondies" in the team, and kept telling them all to "dig in".

Charlie could not understand what he expected from the strikers or which role he should play.

Was he the goal-poacher?

Or was he expected to drop deep?

Charlie had attempted to ask questions but Barney, in a good natured yet infuriating way, avoided answering. It was a muddle.

But it wasn't only the coach's team talk that was worrying.

As far as Charlie could tell, he and Peter were the only strikers on their team and, apart from Joe, none of the rest of the team were any bigger than either of the pint-sized strikers.

And they also had no subs unlike the Reds who

seemed to have plenty of options on and off of the field.

This really was a mismatch on an epic scale.

Once Barney's long-winded talk was over, Joe dragged Charlie, Peter and Michael, one of the boys from their school, away from the rest of the team.

He did not waste his words.

"We are going to get slaughtered. It doesn't take a genius to work that out.

"However we have got one chance."

All three looked at Joe expectantly.

He nodded at Charlie: "Our very own Football Boy Wonder here."

Seeing Michael's raised eyebrows, Joe spoke again.

"No, Charlie is something special. Trust me. We've just got to get the ball to him near that goal. He'll do the rest."

Joe's words spoke volumes, making Charlie feel about ten feet tall.

Joe was a leader, a true captain in every sense of the word.

He was not to be argued with on a football pitch – and Michael knew it. He hesitated for a second before nodding his acceptance.

Happy that everyone was on-board, Joe continued: "We will be under pressure from the off.

"Our only chance is to sit deep and get the ball to Charlie.

"Michael, you play centre-half. Both you and I will look to clear the ball to Charlie at the first chance we get.

"Remember, it's no good knocking the ball over the top because Charlie can't do the running. Ping it straight to his feet.

"Peter, you play as the split striker, dropping into midfield to help out. If the ball breaks loose, pick up the scraps and feed it to Charlie.

"And try to get up the pitch to help him as much as possible.

"Everyone else will be defending and Charlie will need a hand."

Peter gave the thumbs up: "Got it, Skipper."

Joe added: "Leave the defending to us," before turning to the rest of the team and taking up a position in the middle of the team circle.

He could see a lot of nervous faces peering back at him.

Some of the boys were biting their bottom lips, other looking straight at the floor.

Joe's words were short, sharp and inspirational.

"This is our year. Let's not worry about star players or formations. If we believe, we can be a match for anybody. Let's get after them."

Charlie was unsure who started the cheer after Joe's rousing speech but it erupted from their throats together.

Adam and his gang would have a game on their hands at least.

17. THE TRIAL

The Hall Park trials had a number of long-standing traditions.

One was a pre-match handshake, not something Charlie was looking forward to.

Some honoured the tradition. Bishop and Peppermint shook hands and nodded to every one of their opponents as the boys greeted them in line.

The bullies, though, were different.

Adam and Seamus crushed Charlie's hand with venom while Lee opted to sneakily stand on his toe.

Charlie forced himself to block out their childish antics, focusing on the game ahead instead.

But Peter was not so easily intimidated.

When Lee tried the same trick on him, Peter responded by rugby tackling him to the floor.

Barney waded in to separate them – and issued a stern warning as the pair scrambled to their feet: "Any more nonsense like this and you're both out!"

Dusting himself down and rather pleased to see Lee looking furious, Peter jogged over to the centre circle alongside Charlie ready for kick-off.

Most of Adam's team were grinning from ear to ear, anticipating an easy win.

Charlie gritted his teeth.

This was it.

The referee blew the whistle and Charlie kicked off the match he had dreamt about so many times before.

Within seconds, Bishop had robbed the ball off Peter's toe and surged into the Blues' half, sending the ball out wide to Adam.

A casual flick of the boot returned the ball to Bishop's path and the big striker made no mistake, heading the ball into the net past a stranded Joe.

1-0.

Only 15 seconds had gone, the Reds were leading and the Blues had failed to make a single tackle to stop them.

Booting the ball back to the centre-circle in anger, Joe angrily shouted at the defence to wake up.

Barney was shaking his head on the sidelines as the Reds' wild celebrations continued near the corner flag.

They were acting like they'd won the World Cup.

Seeing the sheer over-confidence from the Reds sent a surge of fury through Charlie's body.

He turned to Peter: "Give me the ball as much as you can."

Peter did not argue. He nodded.

They kicked off again but the Reds were soon on the attack once more.

They were showboating, playing fancy back heels and mocking the smaller team who were trying desperately to get the ball back from them.

Within a minute, the ball was being pinged around the Blues' penalty area – and it looked as if the swaggering Reds were certain to double their lead.

This time though, Joe was ready for them.

He anticipated a curling cross from Bishop and cleanly plucked the ball out of the air inches from Adam's head.

In a flash, he threw the ball to Peter who was unmarked near the halfway line, taking the ball in his stride and accelerating into the opposition's half.

The Reds had been so certain about scoring – and greedy for more goals – that they'd only bothered to leave two men in defence.

Charlie was being marked by both of them – Seamus and another lad he did not know.

The stranger left Seamus to mark Charlie alone and headed off to close down Peter.

It was a mistake.

Peter dropped his shoulder and skipped by the defender like he wasn't there, showing he'd lost none of his tricks after his broken leg.

As the last man, Seamus charged towards Peter yelling as he rushed into the tackle.

Peter though was too quick.

Arriving at the ball a split second before his opponent, out of the corner of his eye he saw Charlie was now unmarked.

He slipped the ball through Seamus's legs and sent his friend clean through on goal.

Standing just outside the penalty area with only the goalkeeper to beat, Charlie had plenty of time but he did not need it.

He moved towards the ball, flicked his eyes towards Peppermint's goal, selected the target and smashed the ball with every ounce of power his body could muster.

Boom!

The ball flew like a rocket past the startled keeper into the top right hand corner.

Charlie was so stunned he did not know what to do.

He could hear the crowd cheering and knew Peter had flung himself on top of him, shortly joined by every other member of the team including Joe who had raced from his goal to join in the celebrations.

He had done it. He'd scored at the Hall Park trials.

Once the tangle of legs and arms had sorted itself out and everyone headed back to their position, Charlie turned to the crowd.

His mum was crying with happiness, his dad cheering like a man possessed.

His heart jumped with pride.

He turned back to the pitch, feeling a wet lump land on his neck.

Adam was standing nearby repeating his disgusting spitting trick.

Charlie wiped the saliva away and eyeballed his enemy: "How many goals you scored today, Ad?"

Adam's neck muscle throbbed revealing his hidden anger: "Watch out, Fry.

"It's coming and you'll be crying like a little girl when it does."

Charlie ignored the threats.

He was bored of the bullies – and he wanted more goals.

He wasn't even out of breath; he had scored in the Hall Park trials and he was playing the game he loved.

Something felt different.

He was … confident.

He was playing alongside his two best friends in

the world and he felt brilliant.

They could win this game. All Charlie needed was the ball.

His joy was short-lived as he collided with something solid, nearly sending him sprawling onto the turf.

Seamus had stepped across his path on purpose, driving his substantial shoulder hard into Charlie's chest.

He smirked as the goalscorer went to ground gasping for air.

Charlie told himself to rise above it.

Determined not to take the bait, he showed no reaction, dusted himself down and jogged back to the centre circle.

Peter gave him the thumbs up as they lined up waiting for the Reds to kick off: "Charlie Fry, Hall Park here you come!"

Charlie flushed: "Shut up."

Peter replied: "We're going to beat these boneheads. You wait and see."

18. LEG-BREAKER

Peter, it turned out, was right.

Disgusted they had conceded even one goal, the Reds poured forward into the Blues' half looking to retake the lead.

Lee punted a long hopeful ball forward from the left side in Bishop's direction.

The big striker's touch on his chest was excellent, bringing the ball immediately under control and spinning towards Joe's goal.

His strength helped him to fend off two feeble challenges and move towards the edge of the penalty area.

Bishop shot as Michael threw himself at the ball, making a last gasp desperate effort to stop the shot coming in.

The ball deflected off the defender's outstretched leg and looped up towards the Blues' goal, leaving Joe helplessly stranded.

The ball seemed to move in slow motion as players and spectators watched it spin high into the air, arching towards the unguarded goal.

It clipped the bar and bounced down harmlessly back into Joe's hands.

A groan went up around the crowd at the near miss as both Adam and Bishop stood with their hands on their heads at the Reds' bad luck.

Joe, though, did not wait to milk the moment.

A quick scan of the horizon saw Peter being marked by two players – doubling up on him after his earlier heroics – but Seamus had allowed Charlie to drift away by himself onto the left wing.

With a mighty throw, Joe launched the ball halfway down the pitch precisely into Charlie's path.

Bringing the ball instantly under control with a neat first touch, Charlie turned and began running towards the goal.

Five seconds.

He was one-on-one with Seamus this time although one of the defenders who had been marking Peter was haring over to make the tackle.

Three seconds.

His lungs were beginning to burn, his body screaming for air. He was nearly there, close enough to Peppermint's goal to make the shot count.

One second to go.

Charlie looked up. He was close enough.

A quick flick of his eyes placed the target in the bottom right corner – away from the goalkeeper's left hand.

Seamus saw that the striker was shaping to shoot and stopped retreating towards his own goal.

Charlie could hear the other defender's heavy breathing behind him as he closed in to make the tackle.

It was too late though.

The target locked and Charlie struck the ball with all his might.

Bang!

Both defenders hit him with crunching tackles a second after he released the ball.

Charlie fell to the floor in a mass of legs, watching the ball fly across the ground, straight into the bottom corner of the goal as Peppermint tried desperately to keep it out.

No chance.

The net rippled and the crowd's cheers seemed deafening.

Charlie could barely breathe as he untangled himself from the two defenders, standing wobbly.

Peter was first on the scene to congratulate him: "You did it!"

The rest of his words were drowned out by celebrating teammates, jumping on an exhausted Charlie and slapping both him and Peter on the back.

Against all the odds, they were winning.

The Reds, so cocky and over-confident only moments before, looked shattered.

This time, there were no snide remarks or cowardly threats made towards Charlie or his team.

Just silence.

The referee whistled for kick-off again and it was obvious that the flow of the game had changed completely.

Striding confidently out of defence, Michael robbed Lee of the ball seconds after the whistle had blown.

He slipped the ball square to Peter who had dropped a little deeper remembering Joe's pre-match instructions.

Charlie, still struggling to breathe after his goal-scoring heroics moments earlier, was now being tightly marked by Seamus and another defender.

Peter didn't look to Charlie straight away though.

He skipped past Bishop's half-hearted challenge and burst forward, his legs skimming over the short grass.

A well timed step-over allowed the striker to race away from Adam without breaking stride, heading towards the Reds' goal at pace.

One of Charlie's markers left him to close down Peter, who was threatening to beat the entire team on his own.

Peter waited for the defender to get close before releasing the ball to his strike partner. Charlie knew exactly what to do.

Determined not to allow Charlie the opportunity to turn and shoot again, Seamus was breathing down his neck.

Aware of Seamus's presence, Charlie simply flicked the ball straight back into Peter's path, who had continued his surge into the box.

It was a move they'd practiced hundreds of times at the Rec – and it sent Peter clear.

He didn't hesitate.

He took the ball in his stride and accelerated. Peppermint rushed out to narrow the angle but Peter was calm.

He pretended to shoot and watched the goalkeeper dive to the ground, falling for the dummy.

Peter dribbled the ball past the helpless Peppermint and calmly side-footed the ball into the unguarded net.

3-1!

This time it was Charlie doing the congratulating, finding enough air in his lungs to jump on his friend's back as the crowd cheered.

As the Blues high-fived and celebrated another unexpected goal, Charlie could see many of the Reds slumped on the ground.

Bishop stood on the centre circle, hands on hips looking distracted.

Adam and Lee were arguing with each other.

Barney was dancing on the touchline, his large stomach wobbling like a bowl of jelly as he did a jig of delight.

As the Blues bounced back to the kick-off, Joe reminded them: "Great stuff lads! Concentrate now. Keep it tight, win the ball and our front two will do the rest!"

Joe needn't have worried.

Excited by their unexpected lead, the team tore into the Reds from kick-off, hunting the ball in packs.

The Reds, unsettled and desperate to find a way back into the match, became sloppy in their passing – a far cry from the team that had begun the match.

Another solid tackle from Michael won the ball for Charlie's team and, once more, they counter-attacked.

Michael carefully played the ball into Charlie's feet who laid it off to Peter.

Peter swerved past Lee, who tried to stop him with his arm.

Peter ducked under the foul but struggled to regain his balance.

Crunch!

Peter screamed and collapsed.

19. WALKING WOUNDED

With a face like a mad man, Adam had jumped two-footed in the air straight into Peter's legs. It was no accident.

Charlie froze, unsure what to do.

Peter was crying uncontrollably rolling on the floor and clutching his right leg, the screams piercing the silence that had fallen over the pitch.

Peter's father, who had just arrived at the trial after spending the morning answering an emergency at work, ran onto the pitch along with Barney.

It was clear that Peter would not play any further part in the match. Barney seemed to think his leg was broken.

If the coach was right, it would be the second broken leg in two months for Peter.

Life could be so unfair, Charlie thought to himself as he approached his injured friend.

An ambulance had already been called and was on its way.

Charlie slowly walked over to Peter, whose face was streaked in tears and his hair damp with sweat.

His usual smile was replaced by a look of agony.

Charlie squatted down next to him and ruffled his hair.

"Hang in there, buddy. You're going to be fine."

Peter clenched his teeth and nodded.

"Win this."

The stretcher came on.

As Peter was loaded onto it, Charlie turned to the referee who was now listening to Adam pleading his innocence.

"I went for the ball, ref, and I didn't even touch him.

"He lost his balance and his leg buckled under him.

"I saw it all. I feel a bit sick from being so close to it."

To prove his point, the bully rubbed his stomach, looking sickly.

The ref, it appeared, believed his story and only gave Adam the yellow card warning him: "Any more of this type of behaviour and you'll be off, whether it's an accident or not.

"There's no place in the game for this kind of thing."

Adam nodded.

The ref turned to speak to Barney who had escorted Peter safely to the car park to wait for the ambulance.

The match official did not see Adam wink at Lee and give him the thumbs up.

Charlie knew he'd injured Peter on purpose – but seeing him gloat about getting away with it made him feel sick.

The momentum changed again though with

Peter's withdrawal.

The Blues had no subs so were down to ten men. It was rotten luck.

It left Charlie up front without any real support from the rest of the team.

The game resumed with a free kick for the Blues, which was punted aimlessly towards the Reds' goal.

Peppermint came out and claimed the ball with ease.

Due to his size, Charlie had no chance in the air against the big defenders not to mention the goalkeeper.

Joe saw the problem and barked out a reminder to the team: "Keep it on the floor, fellas! Charlie needs it on the deck!"

With the attacking threat severely reduced with Peter's departure, the Reds' swagger returned and they strode up the pitch with a new-found confidence.

They still kept two men back to deal with Charlie – not forgetting his earlier heroics – but they swarmed over the Blues' defence looking for the goals to get them back into the match.

It did not take long.

Despite Michael heading out a corner from almost underneath his own bar, the ball fell to Bishop waiting on the edge of the box, who curled a shot high into Joe's left hand corner.

3-2.

The Reds began celebrating wildly – all except Bishop who shrugged and refused to return the congratulations of his teammates.

Charlie kicked off and soon the ball was back with the Reds, who were eager to get back on level terms before half time.

The equaliser arrived just as the ref was preparing to blow for the break.

Bishop muscled past two of the Blues' defenders but saw his low shot well saved by Joe.

Unfortunately, the rebound fell to Adam who made no mistake planting the ball firmly into the bottom corner of the net.

3-3.

They were level again.

With a whoop of delight, Adam celebrated by sliding on both knees towards the corner of the pitch as the ref blew for half time.

20. DOWN BUT NOT OUT

Charlie looked around the Blues team as they sat drinking water and attempting to understand Barney's waffling team talk.

They looked a beaten team. They had performed better than anyone could have predicted but they were still going to lose.

Defeat looked a certainty.

Peter's injury plus those two late goals in the first half had changed everything.

Charlie felt bitter. Adam's terrible tackle on Peter had changed everything.

He was a cheat and a liar – and he had gotten away with it as usual.

They were down to ten men and one of their best players – one of Charlie's best friends in the world – was on his way to hospital.

Charlie was feeling shattered, he knew his body would struggle to complete the game.

He had given everything in that first half and had little left.

Half-time was almost finished.

Barney was telling the team to "go out and enjoy themselves" as they hauled their tired bodies from the ground.

Joe helped Charlie to his feet and beckoned Michael to come closer.

"Alright Boy Wonder? This is your moment."

Charlie felt sick. "I'm exhausted. My legs are like jelly. We're going to lose."

Joe and Michael exchanged concerned glances before turning back to Charlie.

"Look, forget about defending. Michael and I will keep them out. That's our job.

"Stay up the pitch and just wait for us to get the ball to you.

"Don't waste energy chasing back, okay?"

Charlie shrugged.

Michael chipped in: "The Skipper is right, Charlie. You've shocked me today.

"You're some football player. We need you. Let's do this for Peter."

Inspired by the mention of Peter's name, Charlie felt a spur of determination run through his aching body.

"Okay boys. I'll give it my best shot."

Their talk was disturbed by angry words being exchanged between the Reds' players as they broke up from their own team huddle.

Charlie looked over at the confusion.

Joe raised his eyebrows watching as Adam and Seamus were being held back by Lee, trying to get to Bishop.

Bishop, who was significantly larger than all three of the bullies, stood and faced them seemingly not remotely bothered by their angry words.

Then he calmly turned his back on them – and the rest of his team – and walked directly up towards a baffled-looking Barney.

Bishop spoke slowly but loudly so everyone close could hear. "Barney, with your permission, I'd like to play the second half for the Blues please."

Barney scratched his head: "Well, son. This is most unusual, I've never known this happen at the trials before. Why?"

Bishop's voice was calm but he seemed to be furious.

"I can't play on that team any longer. I want to win, of course, and have been known to bend the rules on occasion but what happened in the first half was disgraceful.

"I'd rather lose than win like that. They cheated and yet it's the Blues who are being punished by having to play a man short.

"The Reds even have subs so it is completely unequal. That's not right in my book."

Barney smiled: "Welcome to the team, son. You go up front with Fry."

Bishop nodded his thanks to the coach and turned to Joe, Charlie and Mike as Barney wandered over to the referee to tell him about the change.

"Guys, I saw what happened at the Rec the other day. I was on my bike when those morons tried to jump you. They're pathetic."

Joe and Charlie exchanged surprised looks with one another.

"It was you watching in the distance?"

"Yes, I know I should have got involved. I was approaching when Peter arrived to split the whole thing up.

"Then this morning, I find myself on their team and, like Joe, I should have switched immediately.

"But all I could think about was making the Hall Park team. Then I saw Knight spit at you and what he did to Peter, I can't play with them any longer."

The rest of the teams were almost ready for kick-off.

Joe held out his hand to Bishop, who took it.

"Welcome to the team. Now get up front and give Charlie a hand. Let's give them something to think about!"

The boys all broke into smiles.

Bishop and Charlie ran towards the halfway line before the bigger boy spoke again.

"I've seen you practice, Fry. You're the best footballer I have ever seen, professional or not.

"Leave the thugs to me. No-one will touch you this half – just give us some magic."

Charlie smiled. They still had a chance.

21. BOY WONDER

Joe was playing out of his skin.

Without his goalkeeping skills, the Reds would have won the game within the first ten minutes of the second half.

Even with Bishop now in their team, the Blues were under constant pressure.

But Joe had become a one-man barrier performing heroics in the goal including a stunning one handed save to tip Adam's header onto the bar.

Michael was playing exceptionally well too – throwing his body around repeatedly to block shots and crosses as if his life depended on it.

Charlie though had barely touched the ball.

The Reds had reorganised at half-time and had doubled the marking on both Bishop and himself.

Bishop's strength was causing Seamus all sorts of problems, barging into the burly defender and knocking him over on several occasions.

Charlie could not get close enough to him though to link up with him.

His lungs were burning and his head spinning

from a lack of oxygen.

He was a passenger this half, he knew, as the game passed him by.

Peter's injury had delayed their game considerably.

The other three trials had finished and the crowds from those games had drifted over to see the end of the final match.

There must have been almost 200 people watching the game now.

Then the inevitable happened.

It came out of nowhere. Peppermint launched the ball high into the air and Lee rose above two Blues' midfielders to head the ball onwards.

As Adam and Michael raced to get to the ball, the defender slipped at the crucial moment leaving Adam clean through on goal.

Joe flew out of his goal to make the tackle reaching the ball a split second before the opposition captain arrived.

Unfortunately, the keeper's kick flew straight into Adam's outstretched shin, sending the ball back over Joe's head and bounced slowly into the net.

It was terrible luck. The Reds celebrated wildly again, having turned the match on its head once more.

Joe gave the Blues a clap as he retrieved the ball from the net. "Come on Blues! Let's get after them!"

Five minutes to go.

Charlie could feel his anger rising looking at Lee's smirking face as they lined up again. They had been so close but now looked like missing out.

Two minutes to go.

The Reds had the ball and were keeping possession as the Blues chased shadows.

Bishop though was not beaten yet. Snatching the ball with a perfectly timed sliding tackle on Lee, he turned and ran into the Reds' half.

He fed the ball to Charlie, who was hovering on the edge of the penalty area.

The ball came quickly to Charlie though, giving him only a split second to get the target in place.

As soon as he struck the ball, he knew he'd missed.

The target had locked about a metre away from the post – he had rushed it too quickly.

He was right. The ball flew harmlessly wide as the crowd groaned in disappointment.

Charlie shook his head.

The misery of the league was happening again. He was cursed.

Bishop did not agree. "Fry, you'll score the next one. Stay closer to me. You can save us."

Thrilled that a player of Bishop's quality rated him, Charlie felt his chest swell with pride.

Bishop was right; he could do it.

The clock ticked on and they were deep into injury time now.

Joe had the ball and lashed it high up the field in Bishop's direction. The big striker was grappling with Seamus to head the ball.

Charlie watched Bishop slyly nudge the bully in the ribs before the ball arrived. Outraged, Seamus blatantly kicked his opponent in the leg causing Bishop to fall over.

The ref blew for a foul and brandished a yellow card to the big defender.

"Cheat!"

Adam, Seamus and Lee all began complaining

loudly to the ref before shouting abuse at Bishop as he picked himself off the turf.

He winked cheekily back at them and trotted over to Charlie.

"This is all about you now, Fry. Make it count. You're the man."

Charlie felt the butterflies in his tummy return. He gulped down air and picked up the ball.

"You'll bottle it, Fry. You always do." Adam's scrawny voice could be heard above the din of the excited crowd.

Charlie took a quick look at the wall that Peppermint had lined up from the goalmouth before returning his attention to the ball.

He blanked out everything; the miss in the league match, Peter's injury, his argument with Joe, the bullies' taunts and the lightning bolt.

He watched the ball.

"You can do this, Fry-inho!" he heard Joe shout in the distance.

He could do this.

The whistle went and Charlie began running to strike the ball. This time though, he did not look up so the target did not lock.

Instead, he closed his eyes and smashed the ball as hard as he could.

He did not know why he didn't use the target – he just felt it was the right thing to do.

Charlie opened his eyes in time to see the ball fly over the wall and nestle in the top corner of the net.

Peppermint had not even moved.

4-4!

The hat-trick hero was swamped by wildly celebrating teammates.

He could hear the crowd's roar from underneath the pile of bodies.

Struggling for air once more as his team continued to crush him with excitement, Charlie repeated the same sentence over and over again to himself: "That's for you, Peter!"

22. HALL PARK

A week later, Charlie, Peter and Joe were playing football video-games in Charlie's bedroom.

The epic Hall Park trial had been discussed and analysed by the three of them for hours. Charlie's performance had been the talk of the town.

The Football Boy Wonder had become a common nickname for him. It was a little unfair, Charlie thought.

Joe, Peter, Michael and even Bishop had all played their parts in the unlikely draw. Still, strikers always grabbed the headlines as Joe reminded him.

Joe had already been contacted by Hall Park, probably the first name on their list. He would be a Rover next season.

Peter sat with a cast on his leg. He had been terribly unlucky. It was the opposite leg that he had broken earlier in the year.

He too had been contacted by Hall Park coaches.

Due to his injury, he had not been selected for the summer camp but would be invited to attend training once he was fit again.

After all that had happened, Peter was still remarkably upbeat. He kept telling his pals that his time to shine would come soon enough.

Charlie could not have been happier for his best friends but was desperately disappointed to miss out – he could not have played any better.

Deep down though, he knew his lack of running would always be a problem.

He had hoped his shooting skills might win the Hall Park scouts round.

It obviously wasn't meant to be.

"So Bishop got in then?" Joe approached the subject cautiously, not wanting to upset Charlie too much.

"Yes, and Seamus, of course," answered Peter, his eyes fixed firmly on the football video game they were playing.

"Did you hear about Adam?" Joe had obviously been itching to talk about this.

Peter paused the game, his face darkening at the mention of Adam's name.

He was not ready to forgive him for the tackle that had wrecked his leg.

"No. What?"

"He got axed."

"WHAT?!" Charlie and Peter shouted together.

"He was so angry at Charlie's late equaliser that he swore at the referee and Barney too. They don't tolerate that type of thing at Hall Park. He won't be there next season."

"Best news I've heard in a long time," Peter murmured with Charlie nodding in agreement.

Their conversation was interrupted by Charlie's dad poking his head around his bedroom door.

"Charlie? You busy?"

Charlie groaned, wondering what chores he was being recruited for now.

"Dad, I'm kind of busy in this game at the moment."

His dad smiled at his son's reaction. "Okay, fine. I'll tell Hall Park that you're too busy to take their phone call, shall I?"

Charlie's mouth dropped wide open as he scrambled to his feet. "Are you kidding me?"

His dad laughed as his son's obvious excitement.

"No, Boy Wonder, I'm not kidding you. Looks like you've got a busy summer ahead of you."

A SNEAK PEEK

Thank you for reading The Football Boy Wonder – the first part of the Charlie Fry Series.

I hope you've enjoyed Charlie's tale so far.

Please leave your feedback and reviews on Amazon – it is gratefully received.

To whet your appetite, here's a look at the first chapter of the second Charlie Fry book – The Demon Football Manager.

Enjoy and, again, thank you for reading.

**

The website flashed up in front of their eyes.

"There," pointed Joe Foster, unable to hide his excitement at the headline in the middle of the tablet's screen.

"Hall Park Boy Wonder Strikes Again!"
By Andrew Hallmaker.

Joe nudged his friend in the ribs: "Click on it!"

Charlie Fry did as his friend asked, his heart beating like a drum.

Seconds later the article popped up and the two boys leaned forward to read the match report from their game the night before.

Charlie shuffled on the couch before plunging into the article.

"Hall Park's Academy Under-13s won their final pre-season friendly 8-0 last night, thanks to an outstanding display from youngster Charlie Fry."

Charlie's cheeks went red.

The Crickledon Telegraph always seemed to be writing about him at the moment – he wasn't used to the limelight.

The story continued:

"Hunsbury Lakes simply had no answer for the superb footballing display produced by Barney Payne's exciting team.

"Captained by impressive goalkeeping prospect Joe Foster, Hall Park scored twice in the first ten minutes and never looked like losing.

"This was – in the main – thanks to star striker Fry, who scored yet another hat-trick.

"The goals took Fry's pre-season total to 27, which is a new record for Hall Park. He is a player of undisputed quality."

The boys skimmed through the article, flickering over the descriptions of last night's goals.

Both were eagerly looking for same thing – the player ratings.

Charlie scanned through the names. His appeared

at the very bottom – with a man-of-the-match star alongside it.

"Charlie FRY: 10."

Joe smiled and lightly punched his buddy on the arm: "I kept a clean sheet and even get an assist and I only get a nine! I'll beat you one day, Fry!"

Tongue-tied with shyness, Charlie was unsure what to say to his best friend. The praise was almost embarrassing.

The Telegraph kept giving him man of the match. This was the fifth time this month – and the season hadn't even started.

"I ... er ... am sorry. You deserve credit too, Joe."

Joe laughed: "Charlie, you scored a hat-trick! Again!

"I'm teasing you, you silly devil. You need to stop taking it so seriously!"

Charlie grinned at Joe, pushing the short brown hair out of his eyes.

He spluttered a little; it was his lungs giving him a little reminder that he still needed to do his daily physio.

"Charlie, I heard that."

His mum Molly appeared in the doorway looking sternly at her eldest child.

"It's time for Joe to go, I think. It's a big day tomorrow for both of you."

Joe took the blatant hint.

He jumped up from the couch, moved towards the front door and began pulling his scuffed trainers on.

"No problem, Molly. Thanks for having me.

"Charlie, I'll knock for you about 7.30am. Okay?"

Joe didn't wait for an answer.

He gave the Fry family a cheerful wave goodbye as he let himself out, and closed the door behind him with a bang.

Charlie swallowed and realised his throat was dry.

He shuffled the tablet off his lap and scowled at his mum, who watched him head upstairs to begin his breathing exercises.

Having cystic fibrosis was such a drag.

Why couldn't he be like everyone else?

Charlie shook his head angrily as he moved towards his bedroom.

No, he had never ever thought like that – being negative was pointless.

Something in the back of his mind told him it was the nerves.

They had been slowly building up inside him over the past few weeks.

Tomorrow was the big day.

They were starting secondary school.

He had spent almost every waking moment of the summer holidays playing or reading about football – it had been brilliant.

But he couldn't ignore it any longer.

He was going to a new school.

And the thought of such a big change made his stomach flip.

Charlie flopped on to his Blues' bed and positioned himself to begin the exercises that helped him stay out of hospital.

He wondered if anyone at his new school would know that he played for Hall Park. Unlikely, he thought.

How many people actually read the Telegraph or

attended youth matches for the team?

The club was popular, of course, but that didn't mean people at school would know about him or Joe.

Besides, Charlie was still unsure if he wanted them to know who he was or not.

He liked hanging round with Peter and Joe – and he absolutely loved all the football.

However this 'Football Boy Wonder' nickname was a little silly.

It sounded like he was the next England captain or something.

He hadn't even played for Hall Park in a real match yet!

And no-one – apart from his closest friends – knew about his big secret: the magic power that had made him such a footballing superstar.

He smiled to himself.

No-one would be finding out either.

That was one secret that was staying well and truly buried.

Charlie sighed, unable to get rid of the butterflies that fluttered away merrily in his tummy.

He was going to a new school and set for a fresh start – without those idiot school bullies hounding every move.

So why did he feel terrified?

**

The Demon Football Manager is available via Amazon and the Kindle store today.

ABOUT THE AUTHOR

Martin Smith spent more than 15 years working in the UK's regional press before moving into the internal communication industry.

He has cystic fibrosis, diagnosed with the condition as a two-year-old.

The Charlie Fry series is not autobiographical (Martin has never been a footballing great or struck by a lightning bolt, as far as he recalls) but certainly some aspects are based on real life.

Hall Park, for example, has witnessed some of the greatest football matches the world has ever seen.

The Charlie Fry series is about friendship, self-belief and a love of football – a sport that seems to unite people of all backgrounds under one cause.

Thanks for reading. And always, always believe.

Follow Martin on:

Facebook
Facebook.com/footballboywonder

Instagram
@charliefrybooks

ALSO BY MARTIN SMITH

The Demon Football Manager

The Magic Football Book

The Football Spy

The Football Superstar

The Charlie Fry Series is available via Amazon in print and on Kindle today.

Also available only on Kindle:

Charlie Fry and the Penalty Shootout
Charlie Fry and the Grudge Match

And don't miss Martin's Halloween scary story for kids aged 10-14 – if you're brave enough…

The Pumpkin Code

Made in the USA
San Bernardino, CA
26 June 2019